Phanlop the Dragon

Written & Illustrated by M.A.M.

ISBN: 978-0-9980430-1-2

Library of Congress Control Number: 2018964366

Once upon a time, in a magical land far away, the sun shone bright over the lush green meadows. Rolling hills and tender valleys held every creature imaginable. Sparkling streams gurgled over glowing rocks and stones. The sun's warmth chased away the shadows, and the world sang a song of joy. To the animals and unicorns who lived there, it seemed that peace would last forever.

Then, one day, a dragon descended from the heavens and wreaked havoc on the land and its inhabitants. The lush forests were reduced to burnt twigs, and piles of ashes were left where towering trees had once stood. Fire ruled both the earth and the sky. Chaos spread throughout the land.

The oldest and most knowledgeable unicorn, Wise One, recognized the danger from above and knew what had to be done. "Follow me!" cried Wise One.

Wise One led the unicorns and all of the other creatures to a secret valley that the dragon knew nothing about. It was much like the rest of the land before the dragon came. Fields of golden buttercups blanketed the gently sloping hills. Through the middle of the valley ran a glittering river that smoothly glided over rocks. And at the far end of the valley was a waterfall which slowly cascaded down into a beautiful array of colors when the sunlight danced upon it. Here, the inhabitants could see and hear the endless beauty of Mother Nature herself. The unicorns and other animals lived in peace as they shared the tender new shoots of grass.

Many years later, something large blocked out the sun. Colorful scales reflected the sunlight for those below to see. All of the creatures trembled and shook with fear as the whisper of 'dragon' spread around the valley. As the dragon, whose name was Phanlop, approached, the unicorns could see her metallic claws and gleaming eyes quite clearly. Prepared to fight to the end, the unicorns gathered to form the circle of protection over the valley.

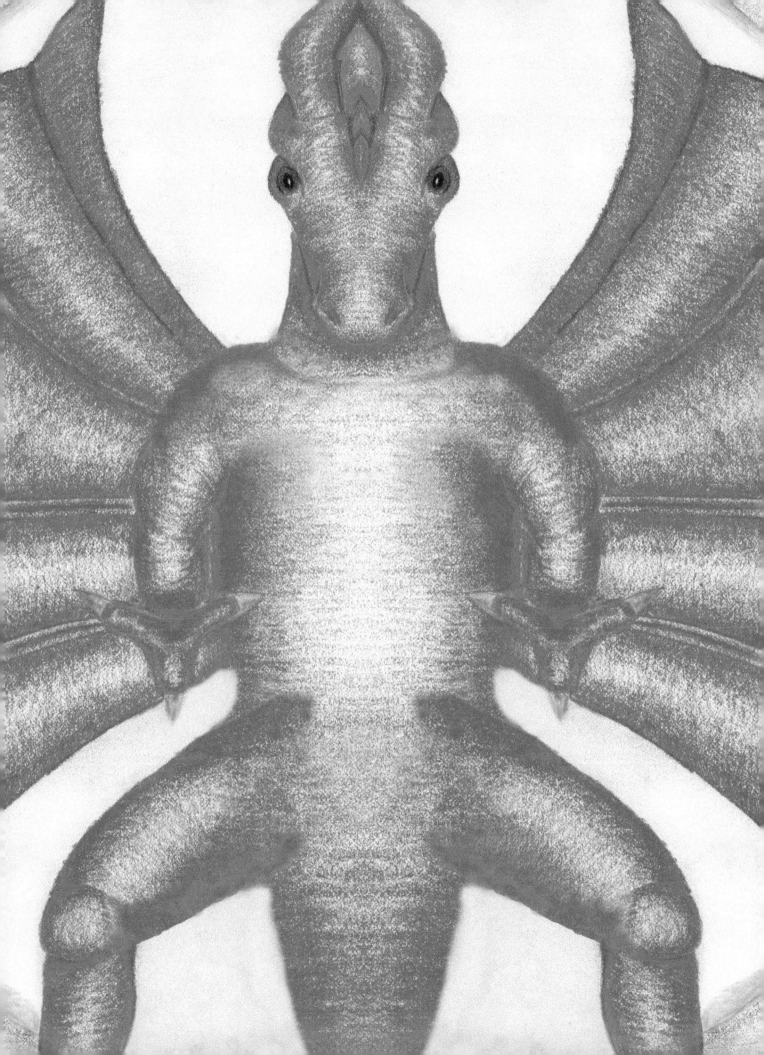

"Dragon," called Wise One, "was our land insufficient for you that now you seek to destroy the quiet refuge that we have made for ourselves? You have ruled over almost all of the mystical lands for many years now. Is that not enough?" Wise One asked. "Why bother us now?"

"I don't wish to bother you anymore," rumbled the dragon. "I only desire your companionship."

"You have deceived us many times dragon, scared both the young and the old, and scarred the mystical lands. What reason have we to believe you now?"

"I have changed," replied Phanlop. "I now see the error of my ways. I was once cruel and heartless," she muttered softly, "but I am different now. I have seen the pain that I have caused the land. Nothing green has grown back. The once sparkling water is now dull and brown. I do not wish to reside in that dead place any longer."

Wise One considered the dragon for a long while before he spoke. "Come back this time tomorrow, and we will give you our answer."

As the inhabitants of the valley watched the dragon fly away, Wise One turned his mind to the problem at hand. The dragon's request was too big for him alone to grant or deny. He thought about what to do. Then, using his magical powers, Wise One sent a message on the breeze, requesting that the unicorns meet at the waterfall. Quickly, the gentle wind traveled through the forest, whispering its contents.

A great meeting was held at the waterfall in the afternoon. All the unicorns arrived to vote on the course of action to be taken. Many of the unicorns objected to letting the dragon come into the valley, while others were undecided. For his part, Wise One only stood and listened. Finally, he spoke to the crowd.

"I believe that the dragon should be allowed into the valley," Wise One said slowly.

"But," cried one of the younger unicorns, "she tried to destroy us before!"

"And she ran us out of our home!" called another.

"Yes, the dragon did do all of those things," replied Wise One. "However, I think that she has truly changed." The crowd was very silent. "Besides," continued Wise One, "I have devised a way to test the dragon." The unicorns nodded their approval.

The next day, Phanlop again arrived when the sun was high in the sky. Seeing Wise One standing on the cliff, Phanlop decided to land beside him. All of the animals gathered on the ledge saw how massive the dragon really was, and they backed away in fright. Wise One, however, was not afraid, and he stood his ground.

"So," began Phanlop, "have you reached a decision? May I stay?"

"Yes," replied Wise One, "you may stay. But," he cautioned, "there is a condition. You must heal the mystical lands."

"Heal the mystical lands?" repeated Phanlop. "But I do not know how!" she cried.

"Do not worry," soothed Wise One, "I will tell you. To restore the land, you must retrieve the jeweled Heart from a cave in the Great Mountain. Legend holds that its power can heal, but only if the creature who holds it is pure of heart."

Phanlop nodded. "I, Phanlop, will go on this quest, and I will restore this land," she vowed. "However," she continued, "I too have a condition. If I am to go on this quest, I need someone to watch over my egg." Phanlop opened one claw to reveal a milky colored dragon egg.

Wise One considered the dragon for a moment. "I will do this for you, Phanlop. Your egg will be safe here. May your journey be speedy." Phanlop took one last look at her egg and flew off into the sun.

As Phanlop flew away from the hidden valley, she wondered if the old unicorn would keep his word. She sighed and turned her attention back to the dead ground that stretched for miles ahead. Below her, Phanlop could see the murky river winding across the barren earth. In the background, the Great Mountains loomed.

Phanlop flew for several days before she reached the Great Mountains. She circled high above them, trying to decide how best to begin her search. Phanlop shivered as she thought, for the air was very cold there, and snow swirled about her. After careful consideration, Phanlop decided to start her search in the highest peak. She landed softly on the peak's ledge and began poking her head into caves. Phanlop spent the whole day doing this. By the time dusk was falling, the dragon was very discouraged.

Just as Phanlop was about to call it a night, something caught her eye. One of the many caves that dotted the mountainside seemed to be different than the others. It was emitting a faint glow, and Phanlop decided to investigate it. As she wiggled into the opening, Phanlop noticed that the walls were speckled with tiny crystals. Never in her whole life had the dragon seen anything like it. Phanlop was fascinated with the colors that seemed to twinkle and light up the night like fireflies on a warm, summer evening.

As the dragon continued down the tunnel, she came to a large cavern. In the center of the cavern sat a glowing object. As Phanlop got closer to it, she realized that it was the source of the light. The jewel, as Phanlop now recognized it to be, shimmered and cascaded shades of soft pinks and reds across the cave walls. It was the most beautiful thing that she had ever seen, even more beautiful than her own egg, and Phanlop knew it had to be the Heart.

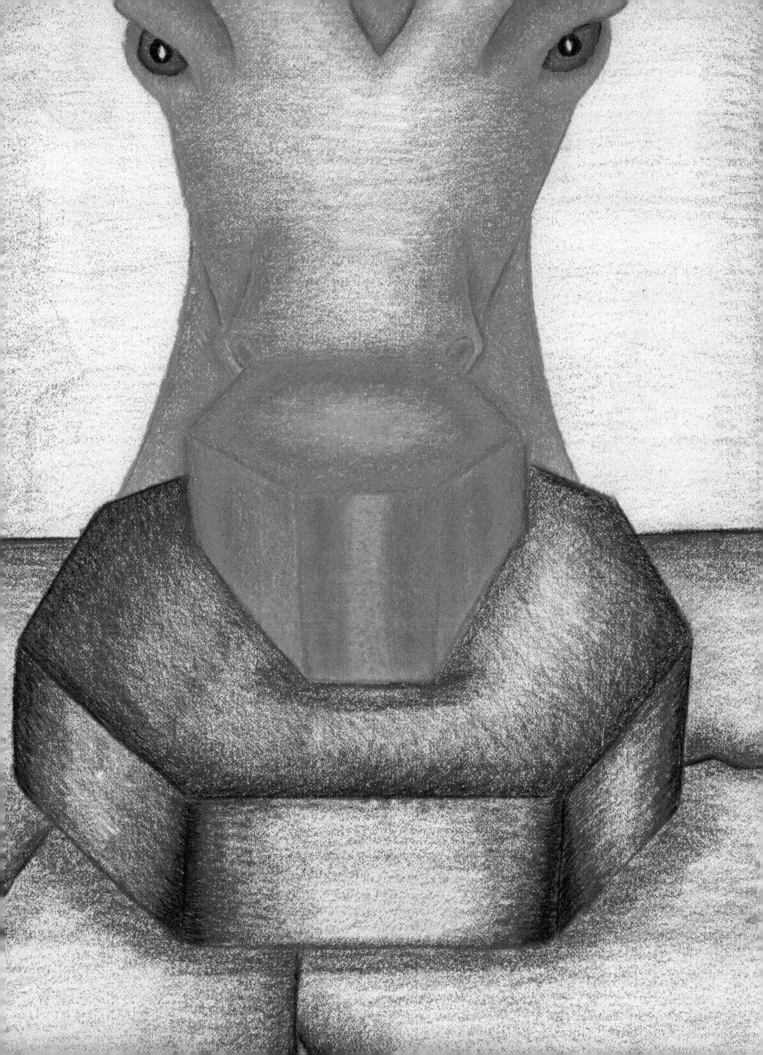

After admiring it for a few more minutes, she picked up the Heart in her mighty claw and began crawling back out. When she finally emerged from the cave, Phanlop was surprised to see the sun out. Despite not sleeping that night, Phanlop decided to start flying back to the secret valley, eager to show off the Heart. As Phanlop flew across the dead land, something strange began to happen. As she passed over the barren ground, green shoots began to appear. Flowers, and even trees, started to emerge from the brown earth, and the stream sparkled again. Even the clouds felt the power of the Heart, and they parted to allow the sun to shine down on the new growth.

When Phanlop arrived back at the hidden valley several days later, she was greeted with much praise. "You have done well," commented Wise One. "You have kept your word to heal the land, and you have done a great deal for everyone in this valley," he paused. "I would be honored to call you my friend," Wise One added.

"The honor is all mine," replied Phanlop. "Besides, I was only fixing what I had done wrong. But please, tell me what has become of my egg."

"I have kept it safe," responded Wise One. "Follow me, and I will lead you to it."

It was an exciting day for all of the creatures because the milky colored dragon egg was due to hatch. Everyone was gathered around the nest to see the miracle that was certainly about to occur. They had waited several weeks for the egg to hatch and had watched it day and night. Never was there a more beautiful day. Beams of sunlight shot through the canopy and danced upon the water. A cool breeze ran through the trees and rustled the tall grasses. Only a few white clouds dotted the nearly flawless sky.

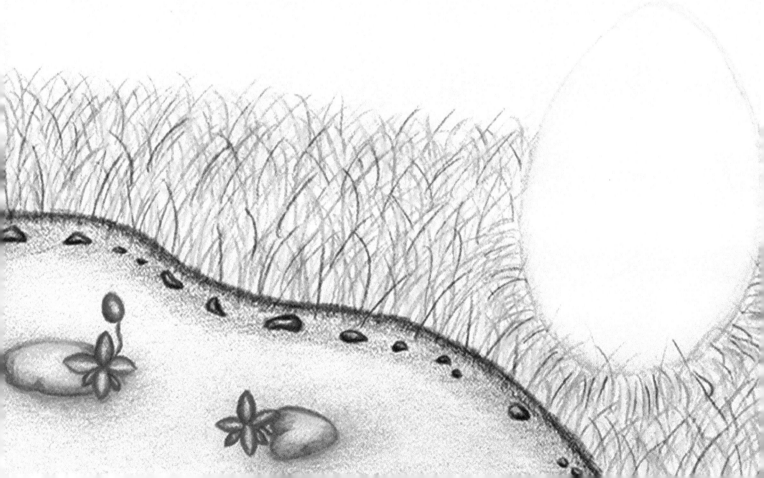

Suddenly, a cracking sound rang out through the air. All eyes were now riveted on the egg. A tiny dragon head poked out of the shell, quickly followed by another. "Twins!" cried the fascinated crowd. The baby unicorns pranced around, giddy over the prospect of not one, but two new playmates.

Each baby dragon was a beautiful turquoise color with golden eyes. They seemed as if they were made from the waters of the stream itself. Phanlop looked on them with proud eyes.

As both the dragon and the unicorns watched the children at play, time seemed to speed up. Before Phanlop or Wise One knew it, the children were grown, and the two friends were watching the grandchildren in the fields. And so it was that the dragons and the unicorns came to live together in peace and harmony. Now, there are more dragons and unicorns than the eye can see, busy frolicking through the fields and across the streams of the mystical lands.

The End

ABOUT THE AUTHOR

M.A.M. is a lifetime member of Girl Scouts of the USA and a recipient of the Gold Award. She enjoys growing orchids and African violets, touring flower gardens, and exploring the National Parks. She is currently studying dog training and loves volunteering with animal rescue groups. M.A.M. currently lives in Ohio with her super cute pup, Valla.

ABOUT ME, VALLA!

I'm an adorable half Chihuahua, half Dachshund pup! Or, if you prefer, a Chiweenie. Even though I'm kind of small, I go on lots of adventures. I can't decide whether parks or food places are my favorite! I should also mention that I do anything I want, like climb on the table, sleep in Mom's bed, and eat food off unguarded plates. As you can tell, I'm the boss, which is why every time someone buys a book, I get a treat. Thanks for feeding me!

CPSIA information can be obtained
at www.ICGtesting.com
Printed in the USA
BVHW021921200120
569978BV00012B/39